ANNE CASSIDY

SPIDER Pie

Illustrated by Bee Willey

PUFFIN BOOKS

For my son Jack

PUFFIN BOOKS

Published by the Penguin Group
Penguin Books Ltd, 27 Wrights Lane, London W8 5TZ, England
Penguin Books USA Inc., 375 Hudson Street, New York, New York 10014, USA
Penguin Books Australia Ltd, Ringwood, Victoria, Australia
Penguin Books Canada Ltd, 10 Alcorn Avenue, Toronto, Ontario, Canada M4V 3B2
Penguin Books (NZ) Ltd, 182–190 Wairau Road, Auckland 10, New Zealand

Penguin Books Ltd, Registered Offices: Harmondsworth, Middlesex, England

First published by Hamish Hamilton Ltd 1995
Published in Puffin Books 1997
10 9 8 7 6 5 4 3

Text copyright © Anne Cassidy, 1995
Illustrations copyright © Bee Willey, 1995
All rights reserved

The moral right of the author has been asserted

Filmset in Baskerville

Made and printed in England by Clays Ltd, St Ives plc

Chapter One

"THE TARANTULA IS in the garage," Jack's mum said as Jack took his school bag off his shoulder and flung it onto the end of the bannister.

"The garage?" Jack Robert's voice lowered into a whisper. He looked around for his dad's coat, but it wasn't there. He wasn't in from work yet. Thank goodness for that.

"Come on. Don't you want to have a look?" his mum asked, walking through the kitchen.

"What time will Dad be in?" Jack said, chewing gently at his top lip, his

I

shoulders hunched with tension.

"Not for another hour or so. Don't worry. Dad never goes out to the garage. I'm not going to tell him. You're not going to tell him. He'll never know that Jimmy's even been here."

Jimmy.

The people his mum worked with had called the spider Jimmy.

Jack followed his mum into the garage. There was just enough light to see. Over in the corner, hidden in the shadow of the stand-up freezer, was the glass tank that held the tarantula.

Jack walked slowly towards it, tiptoeing in case the sound of his feet upset the creature.

"It must be behind one of the leaves, Jack," his mum said, squatting down beside the tank.

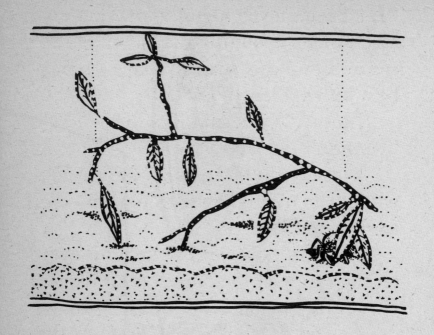

Jack, bending over, looked into the mass of leaves and twigs that filled the glass compartment.

"Perhaps it's asleep," Jack whispered.

"No, no. I don't think so." His mum began to knock gently on the glass.

"It's been moved about a lot. Into my car, along the bumpy roads, out of the car and into this strange space. It may be a bit frightened."

"Jimmy," Jack said in a low voice. "Jimmy."

"You stay here. It will come out in a while. I'm off to play with my new food mixer!"

Jack didn't answer but kept his eye on the inside of the tank. It was like a miniature jungle scene. There were greens and browns and yellows. At the bottom was a lot of earth that had been shaped into small mounds, and some stones. Somewhere among it all was the hairy, black tarantula, the size of an adult human hand.

Jack watched and watched. His eyes grew tired and his back ached a little from bending over.

Was it really in there?

A car door slammed outside and Jack stood upright.

His dad was home!

He was about to turn away and go out of the garage when he noticed one of the leaves moving slightly.

Heavy footsteps sounded up the pathway of the house, but Jack turned to face the tank again.

The tarantula moved slowly out from under the greens and browns, each foot feeling the ground carefully before another moved. Its hair was standing up as though someone had put gel on it.

Jack held his breath. The creature only seemed to move a centimetre every few seconds.

"Jimmy," he said, as the spider suddenly quickened its pace and did a sideways dance across the undergrowth, disappearing underneath a large green leaf.

Jack stood for a minute, smiling. He couldn't wait to show his best friend, Zabeer, his weekend pet!

He was humming as he walked into the kitchen. His dad, his jacket still on, was holding up the box of the new food mixer that his mum had bought.

"Hi, Dad," said Jack, and walked off up the stairs and into his bedroom. When he closed the door he felt his arms and legs explode in a frenzy of movement. All his bottled-up excitement was pouring out.

Finally, when he'd jumped on and off the bed, swung on the coat hooks and done his own personal form of disco dancing, he lay flat out on the floor and looked up at the wall opposite, on which were his various spider posters.

His mum was the best in the world.

Three weeks ago she'd told him about the spider that the school biology department had been given. She'd described it in detail and brought home a couple of photos of it.

He'd always wanted a spider of his own. It hadn't been possible though, because of his dad.

Jack's dad was afraid of
didn't like them at all. Jack
him squealing one evening w
was in the shower. He'd gone to
investigate and found his dad, with a towel over his eyes, pointing towards a large daddy long-legs that had got itself hemmed in in the corner of the shower cubicle.

Jack's mum had elbowed her way in and removed the frightened creature in a tissue. Then she'd taken the towel off his dad and walloped him with it, laughing.

His dad absolutely hated spiders.

That's why his mum had brought the tarantula home secretly, just for the weekend, so that Jack could see it.

It was their secret. Him, his mum and Jimmy.

Chapter Two

THE NEW FOOD mixer was on the kitchen table. Jack's mum was using a screwdriver to fix a plug to it. His dad was sitting at the table, reading the instruction book. Around the machine were various attachments and bowls.

Every now and then Jack caught his mum's eye and gave her a wink. She smiled and then went back to turning the screwdriver. He wondered whether she was thinking of Jimmy, out in the garage, all on his own.

Jack looked at the window. The garden beyond it was so dark it looked as though someone had painted it with a tin of black paint.

"Is there anything you want from the freezer?" he said suddenly. He wanted to check how Jimmy was.

"Er . . . some bread would be nice." His mum's eyebrows had risen at least an inch and her nostrils were flaring mischievously.

"It's too dark for Jack to go out. I'll get it," his dad said, pushing the chair back to get up.

"No," said Jack and his mum together.

"I can use the flashlight. It's OK. You know I always get things for mum," Jack added hastily.

"All right then," said his dad, and putting the food mixer book down, he picked up the newspaper.

Jack took the torch and went out of the back door.

It was pitch black. Only the yellow circle of light from the torch guided him as he stepped out into the darkness. Once in the garage, the beam lit up a long triangle of the floor and the wall. He walked across to the tank. The spider was in full view. Jack bent over and looked straight at it. It had tiny black eyes like small shiny beads and it seemed to be looking straight at him.

Jack knew it couldn't see him very well though. Tarantula's had poor eyesight. He had read it in a book. He had read lots of books about spiders. He and Zabeer had made a Dictionary of Spiders. Under the letter "T" they had masses of information about Tarantulas.

In the morning, Zabeer would come round and see Jimmy himself. Then they could rename him. "Jimmy" was a silly name for such a big spider.

Jack took a loaf of bread from the freezer. Before he went out he looked at the glass tank once more to make sure the lid was on straight. It was.

"Goodnight, Jimmy," he whispered.

The garden didn't look as if it had been painted black, after all. It had been covered with shades of grey. Jack watched as the clouds rushed by and left behind a bright white moon that looked like a hole in the sky.

In the kitchen his mum was just about to turn on the new food mixer. Jack could see that the food compartment was full of left-over vegetables from the previous day's meal.

"I forgot to tell you, Jack," said his mum. "Sarah and Gerry are coming tomorrow. Just for the weekend."

16

The machine started. It made a sound like a cement mixer. Jack looked at the food compartment where all the oranges and greens and whites of the vegetables began to merge and become one colour.

"Sarah and Gerry!" he said with dismay.

"Sarah and Gerry!" his dad moaned, laying his newspaper down.

"Now don't complain, you two. It's only until Sunday. She's my sister and I've said she can come. Look on it as a favour to me. After all, both of you owe me a few favours."

Jack pursed his lips together and looked at the porridge-like substance that his mum was spooning out of the food mixer. It was true. He did owe his mum a big favour. He'd just have to put up with Gerry and her horrible

17

daughter. It was only for two days.

He looked at his dad, whose forehead had a few lines on it. Obviously he owed Mum a favour or two as well.

Jack hated Sarah more than any other person alive. Well, not more than really bad people, or people like the blonde nurse at the dentist, or the school caretaker's son. Or, come to that, not as much as skinny Dennis who lived four houses away.

Come to think of it, he didn't really hate her. He just didn't like her all that much.

Sarah was a brainbox. She was the same age as him and she could say things in other languages, like French.

Sarah's mum had a boyfriend who lived in Paris, and Gerry and Sarah often visited him. He was a games coach, so Sarah had loads of tracksuits and different pairs of trainers. She was very fit and could run faster than Jack.

His aunt was always doing exercises as well. Whenever she stayed with them she usually got up very early and went jogging round the street for half an hour. She was always opening windows as well, saying that the house needed fresh air. Jack and his mum and dad usually curled up close to a radiator and made the best of it.

The worst thing was the cooking. Gerry and Sarah only ate special things that they said were good for them. Gerry usually came with a large bag of vegetables and types of fruit that Jack had never heard of, and spent her time trying to persuade him and his dad to eat some.

This time they arrived at about

nine-thirty. Jack's mum was still in her dressing gown and Jack's dad was still in bed. Jack had already been out to see Jimmy. He was dressed and watching Saturday morning TV.

"Goodness, it's hot in here," Gerry said, giving his mum a kiss and hug. His mum's face had a half-moon smile on it.

"You look well," she said, and
Gerry laughed.

"Healthy living," Gerry said, and
gave Jack's mum a thump on the
shoulder.

Sarah came in carrying a new
rucksack and sat down on the settee.

"You've grown," said his mum.

"Three centimetres!" Sarah boasted,
looking proud, as if it was her doing.

"Say hello to Sarah, Jack." His mum looked sharply at him.

"Hello, Sarah," Jack said in a low voice. Something awful had just occurred to him. What if Sarah found out about Jimmy? Would she be able to keep her mouth shut?

"*Bonjour!*" Sarah got up to twirl around the room a few times.

Then Jack's dad came in, in his dressing gown. Gerry patted his middle and said, "Put on a few pounds since I saw you last?"

"Now, now . . . " His dad put his arms around her and their voices sunk into the back of Jack's head. He found himself looking straight at Sarah.

If Sarah found out about Jimmy she probably wouldn't tell his dad. At least, he didn't think she would.

She would take Jimmy over, though.

She would probably know a lot more about tarantulas than he and Zabeer and the whole of his class put together. Her mum's boyfriend probably had a whole family of them in his Paris apartment. He probably trained them to do tricks.

No, Sarah wasn't going to find out about Jimmy. Jimmy was *his* secret.

"Gosh, it's stuffy in here," he heard Gerry say as she stepped across to the window and shoved it open.

A wind blew in and fidgeted around the room for a few minutes. Then it flew back out again.

Chapter Three

"I WONDER WHY your dad's an
arachnophobe?" Zabeer said, looking
at Jimmy, who had perched on some
branches in a corner of the tank.
"Maybe a spider spun a web in the
corner of his cot one day and that's
why they frighten him so much."

"Maybe," Jack said. "It wasn't a
tarantula, though!"

"What if Jimmy escaped? You might
never find him again."

Jack looked at his best friend with
his mouth wide open, ready to answer
him. But he didn't bother. Zabeer

always thought the worst possible
thing was going to happen.

"Truthfully, it would give one of
your neighbours a fright if they found
this spider in their bath!"

A smile forced itself onto Jack's lips.

"Imagine if it was Mrs Sparks!"
Jack said. She was skinny Dennis's
mum.

Zabeer picked up
an old tea towel
and held it in front
of himself as though
he had no clothes
on. He squealed
and tiptoed from
side to side in
the garage.

Jack's laughter spilled out and he put his hand in front of his mouth to hold it there.

Eventually they both sat down, panting for breath, and leaned against the freezer door.

"Who called him 'Jimmy'?" Zabeer asked.

"The biology teacher at Mum's school."

"What a name! It sounds like someone's uncle."

"Or someone's grandad! It's totally the wrong name for a powerful spider like this. What shall we call him?"

"I know – 'the Terminator'!" Zabeer suggested, and he began firing an imaginary machine gun around the garage.

Jack joined in.

When they'd shot all the brooms

and tools and bits of
rolled-up wallpaper, they
sat down again.

"No," said Jack. "Not the
Terminator. His bite isn't poisonous.
We can't call him that."

"What about 'Alien'?"

"It's not a proper name. You can't
say to someone, 'Hello, Alien, how are
you.'"

"That's true," Zabeer agreed. "How about 'He-Spider'!"

Jack shook his head. It was a difficult decision. They thought about it for a very long while, and in the end decided that Jimmy wasn't such a bad name after all.

"It's tough, like a gangster."

"Like a soldier."

"It's just right," Jack said, and closed the garage door behind him.

Sarah was doing headstands in the garden.

"*Un, deux, trois, quatre, cinq . . .*" she said upside down.

"Hi, Sarah," said Zabeer, "be careful. All your blood could rush to your head and overflow out of your nose."

"Stupid," she sniffed, and then stood upright. "What have you two

28

been doing in the garage?"

Jack and Zabeer looked at each other. Sarah had a horrible way of asking questions. It was as though she knew everything.

"We've got a gang and the garage is our meeting place. We meet there every Saturday morning," lied Jack.

"Not a very big gang, is it?"

"We like it," Jack said.

"Can I join?" Sarah asked, raising her right leg in the air and slowly lowering it.

"It's only for boys," Zabeer explained. "It's tough, you might get hurt."

"*Mon dieu!*" said Sarah, and swiftly brought up her other leg in a martial arts kick. It stopped about four centimetres from Zabeer's chin.

Jack put his arm around his friend's

shoulder and led him into the kitchen.

"That could have injured me!"
Zabeer said, holding his face. Jack
gave him a bit of kitchen roll to hold
against the almost injury.

"Are you coming for lunch
tomorrow, Zab?" Jack's mum said.

"Yes, I think so."

"Good."

Gerry walked in with a giant bag of vegetables and started to unpack them next to the new food mixer. "I'm making my tasty wholefood pie. You'll love it."

Zabeer nodded and Jack led him out to the front door.

"See you tomorrow," he said, and from the kitchen he could hear the chop, chop, chop of a gang of carrots having their heads cut off.

After Zabeer had gone, Jack's mum, Gerry and Sarah got ready to go shopping.

"Whatever you do, don't take the lid off the tank," Jack's mum whispered. "Jimmy's got enough food to last him over the weekend. You can look at him, but don't move the lid."

Jack nodded. He was pleased *he*

wasn't going shopping.

"I'm buying some new jeans,"
Sarah said, following Jack out through
the back door. Jack had his sketch pad
under one arm and a packet of felt tips
in his hand. He wanted to do a really
detailed drawing of Jimmy, one that he
could take into school.

"Jean gave me thirty French francs
to spend!" Sarah added.

Jean was her mum's boyfriend who lived in Paris and who probably had a whole cellar full of tarantulas.

"Thirty French francs to spend on myself!" Sarah said, taking up a ballerina pose.

Jack heard his mum call, "Sarah, we're ready." Then she came out of the back door. Gerry was behind her. "Are you sure you don't want to come, love?" his mum said.

"No, I'm going to do some drawing," he said, and winked his left eye.

"OK. Remember what I told you." She turned back into the house. Sarah had started to run on the spot and with a few tiny steps was inside the back door.

Thirty francs! Jack wondered how much that was in real money. He'd ask his dad after he'd done the drawing.

He heard the front door shut with a bang. He was safe from Sarah for a while. Jack got a stool and placed it a few feet from the tank. He started to sketch a large square that filled his whole page.

He used his green and brown felt tips. He couldn't see Jimmy at all. He was probably under a leaf or a twig somewhere.

When he'd finished his drawing Jack sat down to take a good look. It was accurate. He'd put the leaves in the right places and the twigs showed through. He hadn't drawn Jimmy yet because he was waiting to see him. He knew that the spider would probably start to move around at some point.

He looked closely and saw Jimmy under the same leaf that he'd been under the night before. Not that the spider had much choice. There was very little foliage in the actual tank.

If it had been Jack's tank he would have filled it with strong branches and loads of leaves. In fact, Jack remembered a really sturdy branch that had snapped off their apple tree a couple of days before. He'd been climbing on it and hadn't told his mum because he knew she'd be annoyed.

He went out into the garden and found the branch where he'd left it, over by the rose bushes.

He took it into the garage and held it up against the tank. It was bigger and denser than any of the stuff already in there. Jimmy would love it. He'd be able to make a bigger web and have lots more places to creep in and out of.

Jack stood back for a minute, his heart beginning to beat a little faster.

All he had to do was move the lid slightly, not take it *off*, just shift it to the side a couple of inches.

Then he could slip the branch in. It would just join the others. He could quickly pull the glass back and no one would ever know.

Except Jimmy. He would know and he would be happier.

His mum would never know.

He put the branch down on the floor beside the glass tank. With each hand he took a corner of the glass lid and tried to lift it.

It wouldn't budge. It was heavier than he thought. He got the stool over and stood on it to give himself a better position.

He took a deep breath and lifted the glass.

It moved a couple of centimetres,

and he let it down again to rest his hands and arms.

The third time he picked it up was easier. He was able to get his fingers under the glass lid and move it sideways so that there was a triangular opening big enough to put his hand in. He quickly picked up the branch and began to feed it into the tank. From the far corner he thought he could see some movement from Jimmy.

He only had to push the branch in a couple of centimetres more and then he could move the glass back over to close the opening.

The branch dropped into the tank and fell over on its side. The spider came slowly out of its hiding place and stretched out one of its legs towards the branch. Jack smiled for a minute. It looked as though Jimmy was pointing at it.

"Yes, Jimmy," he said. "It's for you."

He was just about to edge the glass lid back into place when he heard someone calling.

"Jack!" It was his dad's voice.

He turned around and stared at the open garage door. His dad was out in the back garden. In a few seconds he would come into the garage and see the spider!

Jack stepped off the stool and walked swiftly towards the door.

"Hi, Dad," he said, and taking his arm he led him into the kitchen.

"I wondered where you were!" his dad said. "You were so quiet, I thought you must be up to something!"

"No, I was just doing a job for

39

Mum," Jack lied. "Any chance of a drink?"

His dad got a bottle of fizzy drink out of the fridge and began to pour it. Jack was desperate to get back outside, to put the lid of the tank back on straight.

His dad took ages. He undid the bottle-top slowly, and poured the drink straight into the glass so that about three-quarters of it was froth. Then he stood and waited while it all disappeared, and then poured some more in.

Jack chewed his top lip.

When his dad gave him the drink, he swallowed it down in two or three gulps.

"Don't stay out there too long," said his dad.

But Jack was already half-way out to

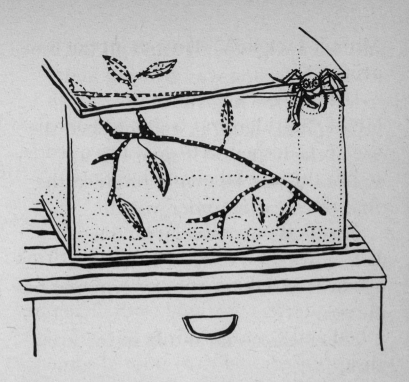

the garage. He ran back to the tank.
The lid was still in the same position,
the branch was still on its side. The
other leaves and twigs were still piled
up inside.

Jack couldn't see the spider though.
It was probably hiding in the
undergrowth. His eyes examined the

tank from edge to edge and all the time
a horrible feeling was growing and
growing inside his chest.

He put his hand in and grabbed the
end of the branch. Using it like a
wooden spoon, he gently prodded the
different areas of undergrowth.

There was no movement. The
feeling in Jack's chest was moving
upwards and seemed to be gripping his
throat.

There was no tarantula in the glass
tank.

The spider had gone.

Jimmy had escaped.

Chapter Four

THE TARANTULA HAD only gone for a walk, Jack was sure.

Jack could find him, if only his feet weren't stuck to the floor.

He could look round for him; behind the freezer, on the shelf with the half-empty tins of paint, if only he could turn his body around.

He could coax Jimmy back into the tank. He wasn't afraid to touch him, to let him scuttle across the palm of his hand.

If only he could stop being a statue and walk across the room.

But he couldn't move. His legs and arms had turned into stone.

Even blinking his eyes was an effort.

It wasn't that he was afraid of Jimmy.

It was much worse than that.

He imagined his mum's face a centimetre away from his. Her eyebrows had grown a few thousand extra hairs and her teeth looked like slabs of concrete.

Her voice would boom in his ears and her finger would point into his shoulder like a red hot needle.

He had to find the spider before she came back.

A car door slammed in the street outside and he jumped. He could move again.

In the distance he heard, "Jack, we're back!"

He looked behind the freezer, under the garden broom, behind the fold-up chairs and on top of the suitcases by the door. He looked inside the empty boxes that his mum kept for rubbish, and on top of a picnic box that they used in the summer. He looked underneath the old rolled-up rug and behind his dad's pile of football magazines.

Jimmy was nowhere.

He heard his mum's voice again: "We're back, Jack!"

He turned a complete circle and quickly looked over everything again. He was just turning away from the door, when a sudden movement caught his eye.

He spun back to the door, but whatever it was had gone.

Jimmy had left the garage.

Hardly breathing, Jack put the glass lid straight on the tank and ran out into the garden.

There was no sign of the spider.

Jack looked to the right and left.

Then he looked again to the left and saw that the kitchen door was open.

He shook his head in panic.

Jimmy had gone into the kitchen.

The tarantula was in the house. And so was his dad!

There was a black spider the size of a furry mitten on Jack's bedside table.

It wasn't Jimmy though, it was plastic.

Jack picked it up and rushed down to the garage. He moved the glass lid again and tucked the spider in under the leaves and undergrowth. Just the edge of one of its legs could be seen poking out. That way, if his mum looked, she'd think the tarantula was still in there.

He had to find Jimmy.

He had to get him back before his dad bumped into him, and before it was time to take him back to school.

But where had he gone?

Jack knew from all his books that Jimmy would look for somewhere dark and quiet. He needed to search each room, one by one.

He started with the kitchen.

Gerry and his mum were fiddling with the new food mixer, slicing a cucumber into pieces in seconds. They each had a glass of red wine on the worktop. His dad was sitting at the kitchen table, slicing up kiwi fruit and putting it into a bowl full of other bits of cut up fruit. Jack looked at him with concern. If he knew that Jimmy was roaming around somewhere, he'd be terrified.

Jack began to look around the room.

He opened the doors of the cupboards, one by one, as if he was looking for something.

"What are you looking for?" asked his mum, picking up her glass of wine.

"Er . . . just something I put away for safe-keeping," answered Jack, his eye searching out the corners of the shelves, in behind the dinner plates and the mixing bowls.

"What?" his mum said.

"Just something . . . it's a secret." His mum looked at Gerry and rolled her eyes.

Jack didn't care. Let her think he was playing a baby game. It didn't matter, as long as he found Jimmy.

"That's me finished!" his dad said suddenly. "I'm off to watch the news."

His dad was going into the front room! Jack hadn't had the chance to look there yet.

He left the cupboards and followed.

Sarah was in an armchair reading a book. Jack tutted. It was typical that Sarah would actually *choose* to read a book!

"What are you reading?" he asked,

keeping his eye on his dad who had clicked the TV on and was sitting in the other armchair.

"It's about aeroplanes," said Sarah. "I'm doing a project on them in school."

"Aeroplanes?" Jack was surprised. He sat down on the arm of her chair. He'd look for the spider in a minute. He was quite interested in aeroplanes himself.

The book was full of pictures and diagrams, and Jack saw a picture of a plane that he had seen a model of in a shop window a few weeks before.

It was a Messerschmitt.

A German war plane! He began to read about it, when he noticed a sudden movement out of the corner of his eye.

He turned quickly and looked over

to the chair where his dad was sitting.
Then it all came back to him. The
tarantula! He was supposed to be
looking for Jimmy.

His dad carried on watching the TV, and Sarah was turning the pages of the book. He could hear her voice, low and distant in his ear: "Here are some other World War Two planes."

Then he saw it.

The spider was creeping along the back of the armchair that his dad was sitting on. It stopped for a second and then moved again. It looked like a gloved hand cautiously moving towards something it wanted to touch.

Jack should have stepped across and put his hand gently over the creature. He should have picked him up and, covering him with his other hand, taken him back out to the garage.

He couldn't move though. His bottom and legs were stuck to the arm of the chair he was sitting on. In his ear he could hear the voice of the television newscaster: jobs lost, British Economy, European farmers. In his other ear he could hear Sarah: early planes, propellers, jet engines.

He could only turn his head. He looked at his dad, then at Sarah, then at Jimmy, creeping along the back of the armchair, just centimetres from his dad's shoulder.

Any minute, its long slender legs would lift and rest on his dad's green jumper.

He should say something. He should warn him.

"TEA'S READY!"

It was his mum's loud voice, the one she usually saved to use in school. It came into the room like a general's command and he, his dad and Sarah all jumped slightly.

His dad stood up immediately,

stretching his arms up to the ceiling as though he'd been asleep for hours.

Jack stood up quickly and tried to look behind his dad to see what had happened to Jimmy.

He thought he saw some movement down the side of the chair, and when his dad walked out of the room, he crouched in the corner, looking.

"What's the matter?" said Sarah.

"Nothing." Jack wished she'd go.

"What are you looking for?" she asked, leaning over him.

Then he saw Jimmy.

He was creeping towards the cupboard where his mum kept all the videos.

"What's *that*?" Sarah had seen him too.

"Sshh!" Jack hissed, and they both watched the tarantula take one step after the other into the black inside of the cupboard.

Jack's right arm slowly reached out and closed the cupboard door.

He heard the "click" of the fastening and sat back.

Sarah sat beside him, her eyes wide open and her hand over her mouth.

"Was that what I think it was?" she said, after a few seconds.

Jack looked at her with dismay. He had no choice now. He would have to tell her.

Chapter Five

JACK WAS IN bed. It was past midnight and he thought that everyone was probably asleep.

First he lay on his stomach with his face in the pillow. Then he lay on his side with his knees bent up. Then he twisted one leg around the other and folded his arms across as though he were a human knot.

Eventually he sat up and clicked his bedside light on.

He couldn't get to sleep.

Everything was a mess. The tarantula was in the video cupboard and had been there all evening. Either his mum or dad or Gerry had been in the living room at some time during the night. He and Sarah hadn't had a single opportunity to get Jimmy out of the cupboard and back into the tank.

At about half-past ten the TV had been turned off and he, his dad and Sarah went up to bed. His mum and Gerry stayed up, chatting.

It could be worse, Jack thought. At least Jimmy was locked in the cupboard, safely out of everyone's way. What if he had been roaming the house?

Jack grabbed one of his pillows and hugged it.

What if Jimmy had crept slowly up the stairs and towards his mum and dad's bedroom?

Jack picked up his other pillow and clung on to that as well.

What if Jimmy had climbed up his dad's side of the bed and made his way under the duvet, somewhere dark and warm?

He dropped his pillows and imagined his dad's sleeping face, and beside it, walking gracefully across the white pillowcase, the tarantula.

"Pss . . . pss . . . " The sound of

Sarah's voice jolted him out of his night-time daydream.

"*Bonne nuit*," she said, and he smiled. Right now, he didn't even mind her speaking in French.

She got on to his bed and put her feet under the duvet. In her hand she had an empty cardboard shoe-box.

"I've got a plan," she said, and he took a deep breath and listened. He felt his shoulders loosening and the muscles in his arms relaxing.

Sarah had been amazed and astonished when he'd told her about the tarantula. She'd kept saying, "A real one? A tarantula spider?", as if there were other sorts of tarantulas.

She'd made him tell her the story over and over, especially the bit where he'd lifted off the lid of the tank. She'd wanted to know all about the spider, where it came from, what it ate, what its habits were. Jack had been able to get his Spider Dictionary out and show her all the information he'd collected.

She'd been impressed.

She'd kept looking over to the closed door of the video cupboard and saying, "*Quelle surprise!*"

Jack knew she wouldn't tell anyone. He knew that she was going to help him get Jimmy back. And here she was in the middle of the night, with a plan.

"Here's what we'll do," she said. "In the morning, my mum usually gets up about seven to go for a run. Your mum and dad will still be in bed. We'll go down, open the cupboard and wait for Jimmy to come out. You can be on one side. I'll be on the other."

Jack nodded his head.

"We'll put the lid of this box flat on

the floor. We'll wait for him to walk on top of it, then I'll place the rest of the box on top of him. He won't be able to move, you see."

Jack began to chew his top lip.

"You can just slide your hand under the lid of the box, turn it the right way up and take it back out to the garage."

Jack looked at Sarah with admiration.

It was a good plan.

It was a great plan.

A few minutes later she went back to her bed and he curled up and went to sleep.

The next morning he felt her shaking his shoulder. He got up quickly and put his slippers and dressing-gown on.

Together they crept downstairs.

It was still dark outside but the

kitchen light was on, so they could see
where they were going.

Jack opened the living room door
and quietly clicked the light switch.
The dazzle of the light made them
both blink for a minute. They stepped
across the cushions that had been left
on the floor, towards the cupboard in
the corner.

Sarah saw it first, and froze.

Jack covered his mouth with his
hand.

They both looked at each other.

The video cupboard door was open.
On the floor beside it was a pile of
videos that someone had been looking
through.

There was no sign of Jimmy.

Chapter Six

JACK AND ZABEER and Sarah sat around the empty glass tank in the garage.

On Jack's lap was the black plastic spider. He had taken it out of the glass tank when he'd shown Zabeer how Jimmy had escaped.

"What are we going to do?" said Sarah.

Jack held up the toy tarantula.

"I don't know," he muttered, his mum's angry face appearing in his mind.

"It might be dead by now, anyway," Zabeer said, his head in his hands.

"What do you mean?" asked Jack.

"Someone could have stepped on him, without knowing. He might be squashed into the carpet."

Jack closed his eyes, not wanting to imagine what a squashed tarantula might look like.

"Or," Zabeer continued, "he might have got out of an open window and been run over by a car!"

Jack looked at Sarah, whose eyebrows were shooting up and down.

"Or," she added suddenly, "he might have been eaten by a cat or dog."

Jack took a deep breath. He imagined skinny Dennis's dog, Rambo, with Jimmy's legs sticking out each side of his mouth.

"I'll never speak to that dog again," Jack said, standing up. The plastic spider dropped off his lap on to the ground, and Zabeer and Sarah jumped as though it was the real Jimmy and not a toy.

It sat lifeless on the floor between them.

"He's probably not dead at all," Jack said, not really believing it.

"No," agreed Zabeer, nodding his head rapidly, "just hiding somewhere."

"All we've got to do is find him," said Sarah, pulling a piece of her hair into the side of her mouth.

"Let's take one room at a time. We could start upstairs and work down," Zabeer suggested.

"No, we saw him downstairs last. Let's start with the kitchen," argued Sarah.

"Right," said Jack, "this is what

we'll do. We'll all sit in the kitchen. Gerry won't mind. She's making the wholefood pie. She likes to chat. Now you, Zab, you keep your eye on the ceiling area. Sarah, you look around the floor, and I'll look along the worktops. If he's there, one of us will see him. OK?"

"Yessir!" Zabeer stood up and saluted.

"*Oui, mon capitaine*!" Sarah stood upright with her arms at her sides.

"Forward, men," said Jack, and the three of them marched out of the garage.

In the kitchen, Gerry was chopping up vegetables for the pie. On the table in front of her were dozens of carrot slices and some orange and green cubes that could have been swedes or turnip. It

all looked like a great pile of miniature
building bricks, waiting to be played
with. Beside it, on a plate, were six
skinned tomatoes. Jack thought they
looked like tiny red balloons that had
lost their air and floated to the ground.

Gerry was humming a song.

On the work surface behind her was

the food mixer, waiting to be used.

Sarah was chatting about her gym class. For once Jack didn't mind. He knew she was only doing it to keep Gerry occupied, while the rest of them looked for Jimmy.

"Soon I'll be in the senior gym team, shan't I, Mum?"

Jack looked along the worktop. His eye traced the line along the top of the wooden cutting board, past the electric kettle and up to the toaster. Then he switched to the other end and started at the jars that held the tea bags and coffee, past the mug-tree and in front of a big green plant.

"Then I'll have to have a whole new set of leotards, shan't I, Mum?" Sarah was continuing. Jack glanced at her for a moment and saw her looking along the ground as she was speaking. He quickly looked at Zabeer, whose head was bent back so that he could look at the ceiling.

"Only if we've got the money," Gerry replied, turning back to the food mixer. "We'll see.' She began to grab handfuls of the vegetables and drop them into the food mixer. First the carrots, then the orange and green bits.

"You said we did have the money!" Sarah's voice had risen. Jack turned around to look at her. She was standing up and had one hand on her hip and the other on her forehead.

"Don't – raise – your – voice – please – Sarah." Gerry spoke quietly and slowly, each word sounding like the last she would ever speak.

Sarah inhaled loudly, looking straight at her mother. Jack tried to make a face at her. This wasn't a good time to have a row, not while they were still looking for Jimmy.

"Jean will buy it for me!" Sarah said crossly. Jack clenched his fists and willed Sarah to look at him so that he could remind her about what they were doing. She didn't look at him though, she was looking straight at her mum.

"Will he now?" Gerry said, picking up the plateful of skinned tomatoes and tipping it onto the vegetables. She stopped, her hand picking up the lid, and turned back to her daughter. "Just because your friends are here, there is no need to show off, Sarah. We'll discuss this later."

Zabeer was making hand signals at Jack. What did he want? Jack screwed his face up at him. Couldn't he see that Jack was trying to attract Sarah's

attention, so they could continue looking for Jimmy?

"Jean is not made of money and neither am I," Gerry said sharply.

Zabeer was pointing frantically at Jack, or at least in his direction.

What on earth was he doing? Had he forgotten that they were looking for the tarantula?

Then it came to Jack. Zabeer had seen the spider. He turned slowly around and looked behind him.

There on the worktop was Jimmy.

"What about your music lessons? Your dance class? Your computer games?" Gerry continued. "They all cost money." But Sarah wasn't listening. She had seen Jimmy too.

Jack, frozen to the spot, watched the spider creep across the worktop and up the side of the food mixer. He opened

his mouth to cry out, but the words were
made of lead and wouldn't come. The
creature reached the top of the bowl and
then gracefully dropped inside.

That was when Gerry lost her
temper.

"You think you know it all, young
lady, don't you?" she said, her voice
loud and angry. She turned away from

Sarah and back to the food mixer. In her hand she had the lid.

She was going to put it back on the machine!

Jack looked frantically at Zabeer, whose mouth was hanging open like a tunnel that a train might go into. He tried to say something again, but the words had sunk even further down inside him.

She was going to put the lid on and start the mixer!

Jack couldn't look.

He couldn't watch.

He closed his eyes.

There was silence for a few seconds.

Then the 'vrrrmmmm'' of the machine.

He felt faint and put his hand out to hold on to a chair.

Eventually, after what seemed like a

hundred minutes, Jack opened his eyes.

Sarah and Zabeer and he looked at the machine. There were reds and browns and greens swirling together.

"What's the matter with you lot?" Gerry said.

"Nothing," Jack gasped, finding his voice. Inside, an invisible hand grabbed his stomach and twisted it round.

"You'll get your leotard when I say so, Sarah, and not before," Gerry said, picking up a lump of pastry and slapping it down on the table.

"Leotard?" Sarah was still looking at the food mixer. She turned to Jack and Zabeer, a look of shock on her face, and said, "What leotard?"

Jack didn't answer. He turned and went upstairs to his bedroom. Zabeer followed him in silence.

78

Chapter Seven

THE FAMILY SAT down at the dinner
table.

Gerry came into the room and
placed the pie in the middle of the
tablecloth.

The spider pie.

Jack looked at it with horror.

On the outside it looked the same as
any other pie. It had a light brown
crust and seemed to rise up in the
middle.

"Mm!" said Jack's dad, his hand
moving in circles on his stomach.

"This looks wonderful," agreed his

mum, taking a bottle from the side and pouring it into glasses.

"It's usually very tasty," Gerry said, standing back, a tea towel in each hand, "and full of good things!"

Jack's dad laughed out loud, then he stopped and looked over at Jack and Zabeer and Sarah.

"What's the matter with you lot? Have your tongues gone on strike!" He laughed again before taking a sip from his glass.

"Have you had a quarrel?" asked

Gerry, picking up a large knife from the table.

"No," said Jack and Zabeer. Sarah said nothing.

"Are you still sulking, Miss?" Gerry gave Sarah a look that said, wait till I get you on your own.

"No," Sarah said, her face pale and her teeth clenched. She looked very unhappy.

So she should, Jack thought. It was all her fault. If she hadn't got carried away, going on about her leotards and

her gym class, Jimmy would still be alive. He might be back in his tank at this very minute.

Now he was inside the pie.

In a few minutes he would have some of it on his plate.

He looked at Zabeer.

"I knew something like this would happen," Zabeer hissed between his teeth.

Jack's mum raised her eyebrows. "Pardon?"

"I'm . . . not really very hungry," Zabeer said, holding his fork in mid-air.

"I won't give you very much then," said Gerry, cutting into the pie and scooping out a giant bit for Jack's dad. Then she served the rest of the portions.

In front of Jack was a small triangle

of pastry that sat on top of a steaming mixture of red, yellow, orange and green lumps.

He picked up his fork and scooped a bit onto it. He moved it from one side of the plate to another, and then pushed it around the edge.

"Jack!" He heard his mum's warning voice. In a few seconds he would have to pick up a forkful of the pie and put it into his mouth.

He looked at Zabeer, and then at Sarah. Both of them were drinking their glasses of orange and looking at him to see what he was going to do.

He couldn't put the mixture into his mouth. He would have to own up and tell his mum. He would have to confess. He opened his mouth to speak, when something black moved at the corner of his eye. He turned his head to look.

Over there, along the window ledge, was Jimmy.

Jack closed his eyes. Was he imagining things? He opened them again.

Jimmy was still there, his legs

moving slowly. He was heading towards the brown velvet curtains.

Jack put the forkful of Gerry's pie into his mouth and nudged Sarah with his leg and Zabeer with his elbow.

The three adults were busy talking. Sarah and Zabeer looked across to the window and saw the tarantula.

Jack chewed the pie and swallowed. Now was the time for him to get up and go over and get the spider, but his bottom wouldn't move. His legs felt as though they were tied to the chair.

His mum and dad and Gerry had their backs to the window, but at any minute one of them could turn round.

Zabeer and Sarah were looking at him.

He should get up.

Instead, Sarah stood up and picked up one of the tea towels. Without a word she walked across to the window ledge, dropped the towel on to the spider and gently picked it up.

She held it close to her chest while Zabeer and Jack looked at her with their mouths open.

The adults turned around to see what she was doing.

"It's just a daddy-long-legs," she said, "I know Uncle doesn't like them," and walked out of the room.

A few seconds later Jack heard the back door slam.

"Any more pie?" said Gerry.

Chapter Eight

"I THOUGHT YOU said you saw it go into the mixer!" said Zabeer.

"I did. I was sure I had!" And then Jack remembered.

He'd closed his eyes because he couldn't bear to look.

In those few seconds, before Gerry screwed the lid on, Jimmy must have scuttled out of the mixer bowl and back behind the cups and jugs on the worktop.

Jack, Zabeer and Sarah were sitting around the tank. Inside, Jimmy was creeping up and down the new branch that Jack had put in.

"I think he's brilliant. I wish I had a tarantula," Sarah said.

"After today, I don't think I ever want to look at another spider again!" Zabeer said.

Jack didn't say anything, but he felt like that too.

Later Zabeer went home and Sarah and Gerry began to get ready to go.

Jack went into his bedroom and looked at all his pictures of spiders and his Spider Dictionary.

Sarah had saved the day. She had been the quick-thinking one who had got up and captured Jimmy. Jack decided that he ought to give her something.

As she and Gerry were packing

stuff into their car,
he handed her the
Spider Dictionary that he and
Zabeer had made.

"*Magnifique*!" said Sarah, smiling.
She wasn't so bad, for a girl.

In his bedroom Jack got a large
piece of card and wrote on it,
DICTIONARY OF AEROPLANES.

It was time to move on to something
new.

READ MORE IN PUFFIN

For children of all ages, Puffin represents quality and variety – the very best in publishing today around the world.

For complete information about books available from Puffin – and Penguin – and how to order them, contact us at the appropriate address below. Please note that for copyright reasons the selection of books varies from country to country.

On the worldwide web: www.penguin.co.uk

In the United Kingdom: Please write to *Dept. EP, Penguin Books Ltd, Bath Road, Harmondsworth, West Drayton, Middlesex UB7 ODA*

In the United States: Please write to *Consumer Sales, Penguin USA, P.O. Box 999, Dept. 17109, Bergenfield, New Jersey 07621-0120*. VISA and MasterCard holders call 1-800-253-6476 to order Penguin titles

In Canada: Please write to *Penguin Books Canada Ltd, 10 Alcorn Avenue, Suite 300, Toronto, Ontario M4V 3B2*

In Australia: Please write to *Penguin Books Australia Ltd, P.O. Box 257, Ringwood, Victoria 3134*

In New Zealand: Please write to *Penguin Books (NZ) Ltd, Private Bag 102902, North Shore Mail Centre, Auckland 10*

In India: Please write to *Penguin Books India Pvt Ltd, 706 Eros Apartments, 56 Nehru Place, New Delhi 110 019*

In the Netherlands: Please write to *Penguin Books Netherlands bv, Postbus 3507, NL-1001 AH Amsterdam*

In Germany: Please write to *Penguin Books Deutschland GmbH, Metzlerstrasse 26, 60594 Frankfurt am Main*

In Spain: Please write to *Penguin Books S. A., Bravo Murillo 19, 1° B, 28015 Madrid*

In Italy: Please write to *Penguin Italia s.r.l., Via Felice Casati 20, I–20124 Milano*

In France: Please write to *Penguin France S. A., 17 rue Lejeune, F–31000 Toulouse*

In Japan: Please write to *Penguin Books Japan, Ishikiribashi Building, 2–5–4, Suido, Bunkyo-ku, Tokyo 112*

In South Africa: Please write to *Longman Penguin Southern Africa (Pty) Ltd, Private Bag X08, Bertsham 2013*